Three Little Kittens

and friends

Miles Kelly

First published in 2011 by Miles Kelly Publishing Ltd
Harding's Barn, Bardfield End Green, Thaxted, Essex, CM6 3PX, UK

2 4 6 8 10 9 7 5 3 1

Editorial Director Belinda Gallagher
Art Director Jo Cowan
Editor Sarah Parkin
Cover/Junior Designer Kayleigh Allen
Production Manager Elizabeth Collins
Reprographics Stephan Davis, Ian Paulyn

ISBN 978-1-84810-407-5

Printed in China

British Library Cataloguing-in-Publication Data
A catalogue record for this book is available from the British Library

ACKNOWLEDGEMENTS

Artworks are from the Miles Kelly Artwork Bank
Cover artist: Denise Coble

Made with paper from a sustainable forest

www.mileskelly.net
info@mileskelly.net
www.factsforprojects.com

Self-publish your
children's book

buddingpress.co.uk

Contents

Head, Shoulders, Knees and Toes

Head, shoulders, knees and toes,
Knees and toes,
Head, shoulders, knees and toes,
Knees and toes,
And eyes and ears and mouth and nose,
Head, shoulders, knees and toes,
Knees and toes.

Touch each part of the body as you sing the rhyme.

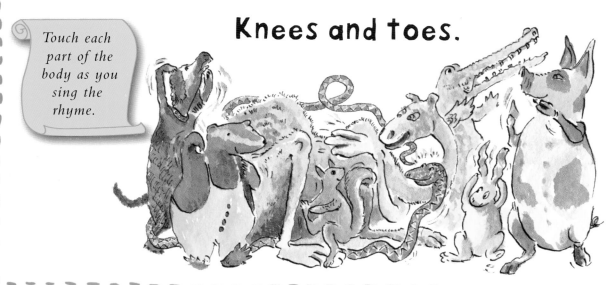

Pussy Cat, Pussy Cat

Pussy cat, pussy cat,
where have you been?
I've been to London to look at
the queen.
Pussy cat, pussy cat,
what did you there?
I frightened a little mouse
under her chair.

Who Killed Cock Robin?

Who killed Cock Robin?
"I," said the sparrow,
"With my bow and arrow,
I killed Cock Robin."

Who saw him die?
"I," said the fly,
"With my little eye,
I saw him die."

Who caught his blood?
"I," said the fish,
"With my little dish,
I caught his blood."

Who'll dig his grave?
"I," said the owl,
"With my spade and trowel,
I'll dig his grave."

Who'll be the clerk?
"I," said the lark,
"If it's not in the dark,
I'll be the clerk."

Who'll be the parson?
"I," said the rook,
"With my little book,
I'll be the parson."

Who'll sing a psalm?
"I," said the thrush,
As she sat on a bush,
"I'll sing a psalm."

Who'll be chief mourner?
"I," said the dove,
"I mourn for my love,
I'll be chief mourner."

Who'll toll the bell?
"I," said the bull,
"Because I can pull,
I'll toll the bell."

All the birds of the air
Fell sighing and sobbing,
When they heard the bell toll
For poor Cock Robin.

To all it concerns,
This notice apprises,
The sparrow's for trial
At the next bird assizes.

Diddle, Diddle, Dumpling

Diddle, diddle, dumpling,
My son John,
Went to bed with his
Trousers on;
One shoe off,
And one shoe on,
Diddle, diddle, Dumpling,
My son John.

Cinderella

A retelling from the original tale
by Charles Perrault

Once upon a time, when fairy godmothers still existed, there was a girl called Cinderella. She lived with her father and his new wife, and her two new stepsisters. The stepmother did not like Cinderella very much, mostly because she was so much nicer than her own two daughters. Cinderella was also much prettier. Oh, but the stepsisters were ugly!

Cinderella had to do all the work in the

house as the ugly sisters were also very lazy. They spent all the father's money on new clothes and endless pairs of shoes, and then went off to parties leaving poor Cinderella with piles of stockings to mend.

One day a very grand invitation arrived. The prince was looking for a wife, and had decided to give a ball in three days' time for all the young ladies in the land. The ugly sisters could talk about nothing else. They bought lots of new dresses and many pairs of matching shoes, and then spent every hour trying them all on. They made Cinderella curl their hair and iron their ribbons and powder their noses. Cinderella was so exhausted running around after them that she had no time to look into her own wardrobe to choose what she should wear.

In a waft of perfume, the ugly sisters swept out of the door into the carriage without as much as a thank you to Cinderella. She closed the door sadly, and went to sit by the fire in the kitchen.

"I wish I could have gone to the ball, too," she sighed.

There was a sudden swirl of stars, and there in front of Cinderella stood an old lady with a twinkle in her eye, and a wand in her hand.

"You shall go to the ball, my dear Cinderella. I am your fairy godmother," she said, smiling. "Now, we must be quick, there is much to do! Please bring me a large pumpkin from the vegetable patch. Oh, and six mice from the barn, and you will find four lizards by the water butt."

Cinderella did as she was bid. With a wave of the wand, the pumpkin was turned into a glittering golden coach and the mice into six pure white horses. The lizards became elegant footmen, dressed in green velvet.

"Now you, my dear," said the fairy godmother, turning to Cinderella. A wave of the wand, and Cinderella's old apron disappeared and there she stood in a white dress, glittering with golden stars. Her hair was piled on top of her head and it too was

sprinkled with stars. On her feet were tiny glass slippers with diamonds in the heels.

"Enjoy yourself, my dear," said the fairy godmother, "but you must leave before midnight for then my magic ends and you will be back in your old apron with some mice and lizards at your feet!"

When Cinderella arrived at the ball everyone turned to look at this unknown beauty who had arrived so unexpectedly. The prince hurried over to ask her to dance and then would not dance with anyone else all evening. The ugly sisters were

beside themselves with rage, which of course made them look even uglier.

Cinderella was enjoying herself so much that she forgot the fairy godmother's warning, so she had a terrible fright when the clock began to strike midnight. She turned from the prince with a cry and ran down the stairs of the palace into her carriage, and disappeared as suddenly as she had arrived. One of the tiny glass slippers with diamonds sparkling in the heels had slipped from her foot as she ran. The prince picked it up and turning to the crowded ballroom declared, "I shall marry the girl whose foot fits this slipper!"

Cinderella, meanwhile, had just managed to reach her garden gate when all her finery disappeared, and by the time the ugly sisters arrived home, both in a towering rage, she was sitting quietly by the fire.

The next morning, the prince went from house to house looking for the mystery girl whose foot would fit the glass slipper. But no one had feet that small. He reached Cinderella's house where first one ugly sister and then the next tried to squash her big feet into the slipper.

"Please let me try," said a quiet voice from the corner, and Cinderella stepped forward. The sisters just laughed in scorn but they soon stopped when they saw that the tiny slipper fitted Cinderella perfectly.

There was a sudden swirl of stars, and there in front of Cinderella stood her fairy godmother with a twinkle in her eye, and a wand in her hand. In an instant, Cinderella was clothed in a gorgeous dress of cornflower blue silk decorated with pearls. On her feet she wore white boots with blue tassels.

The prince whisked Cinderella off to the palace to meet the king and queen, and the wedding took place the very next day. Cinderella forgave the ugly sisters, she was that sort of girl. But the prince insisted the sisters spent one day a week working in the palace kitchens just to remind them how horrid they had been to Cinderella.

Three Little Kittens

Three little kittens,
They lost their mittens,
And they began to cry,
"Oh, mother dear, we sadly fear
That we have lost our mittens."
"What! Lost your mittens,
You naughty kittens!
Then you shall have no pie.
Mee-ow, mee-ow, mee-ow.
No, you shall have no pie."
The three little kittens,
They found their mittens,
And they began to cry,

"Oh, mother dear, see here, see here,
For we have found our mittens."
"What! Found your mittens,
You silly kittens!
Then you shall have some pie."
"Purr-r, purr-r, purr-r,
Oh, let us have some pie."

I always Eat my Peas with Honey

I always eat my peas with honey,
I've done it all my life.

They do taste kind of funny
but it keeps them on my knife.

Anonymous

I Love Little Pussy

I love little pussy,
Her coat is so warm,
And if I don't hurt her,
She'll do me no harm.
So I'll not pull her tail,
Nor drive her away,
But pussy and I very gently will play.
I'll sit by the fire,
And give her some food,
And pussy will love me because
I am good.

Jumping Joan

Here I am,
Little Jumping Joan;
When nobody's with me
I'm all alone.

The Emperor's New Clothes

Retold from the original tale
by Hans Christian Andersen

There was once an emperor who loved new clothes above everything else. Designers, tailors, clothmakers and dyer travelled to his city from all over the world. Anyone who could suggest flashy, fancy new outfits for the emperor was always welcome at the palace.

One day, it was the turn of two weavers

to be ushered into the emperor's dressing room. The emperor, his butler and all his Officers of the Royal Wardrobe, gasped with amazement as they listened to them describe their work.

"We have created a special fabric that is so light and airy the wearer cannot feel it," the first weaver announced.

"Our samples are top secret, which is why we have not been able to bring any to show you," the second weaver explained.

"However we can assure you that not only are our designs and patterns beautiful," said the first weaver, "but the fabric has the unique advantage that it is completely invisible to anyone not worthy of his job –"

"– or who is just plain stupid!" laughed the second weaver. The emperor and all his courtiers gasped and chuckled along.

"We would be honoured if you would like to order the very first suit made out of this extraordinary fabric, your majesty," said the first weaver, bowing low.

The emperor clapped his hands with delight.

"I'd like to place an order right away!" he commanded, and he gave the two weavers a large sum of money so that they could buy the rare, expensive materials they needed and begin their work without delay.

The weavers set up their looms in the palace studio and started work immediately. News of the strange cloth spread around the city like wildfire and soon everyone was talking about it. But the weavers worked behind closed doors and no one got even a glimpse of what they were doing. Still, day and night everyone heard the looms clicking and the shuttles flying,

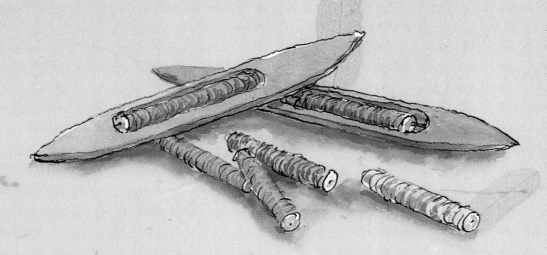

and work on the magical cloth seemed to
be progressing well.

As the days went on, the emperor began
to feel rather uneasy about seeing the cloth
for the first time. 'Imagine if I can't see the
fabric,' he thought. The worried emperor
decided to send his trusted butler to see how
the weavers were getting on. He was sure
that his butler was both fit for his job and
very wise, and would be sure to see the
wonderful material.

The weavers bowed low and ushered the
butler into the studio. But the butler
couldn't see anything at all. 'Heavens
above!' the butler thought. 'Those looms

look totally bare to me! I must either be a very bad butler, or else I'm an idiot. No one must ever find out . . .'

So he praised the material that he could not see, told the king that the weavers' work was magnificent, and everyone in the city heard that the cloth was truly unbelievable!

Soon afterwards, the weavers sent word to the emperor that they needed more money

to buy essential items for the work. The emperor had been so delighted with the butler's report that he sent them twice as much money as before. The emperor was more excited than ever. "I'm going to have the most amazing suit of clothes in the world!" he said to himself.

Eventually, just as the emperor thought he was going to explode with waiting, the weavers announced their work was finished. They went to the dressing room to present the material to the emperor amid fanfares of trumpets. "Is the cloth not beautiful beyond all imagining?" the weavers sighed.

The emperor smiled a wide smile, trying to hide his horror. All that the weavers appeared to be holding up before him was thin air. The emperor's worst fear had come true — to him the cloth was invisible! 'I cannot be thought to be a fool or not worthy to be ruler,' the despairing emperor thought. So he beamed and leant forwards and inspected the air. "Wonderful! Splendid! Magnificent!" he cried, and his butler and all the Officers of the Royal Wardrobe nodded and cried out compliments. None of them could see anything either, but they weren't about to risk losing their jobs by admitting it.

So the weavers got out their tape measures and their scissors and they set about cutting the thin air (or so it seemed) into a pattern. All night long they sewed with needles that appeared to have no thread, and in the morning they announced that the emperor's new clothes were ready. "If your majesty would care to disrobe, we will dress you in the amazing garments."

The emperor swallowed hard and took off all his clothes. The weavers helped him on with the underpants, trousers, shirt and jacket that he couldn't see. "Aren't they lighter than cobwebs?" they sighed. The emperor spluttered his agreement. He didn't feel like he had any clothes on at all.

The emperor stood back and looked at himself in the mirror. According to what he saw, he didn't have a stitch on! But he turned this way and that, pretending to admire himself. The butler and all the Officers of the Royal Wardrobe cried out, "How wonderfully the new clothes fit you!" and "We have never seen such amazing colours!" and "The design is a work of genius!" – even though it looked to them as if the emperor was as naked as the day he was born.

'Everyone else can see my new suit except me,' the emperor thought to himself glumly. And he walked out of the palace to parade before the people in his new clothes.

The streets were lined with hundreds of people who ooohed! and aaaahed! over the emperor's invisible new clothes — for none of them wanted to admit that they couldn't see them.

Suddenly, a little boy's shrill voice rose over the applause of the crowd. "But the emperor has nothing on!" the child shouted. "Nothing on at all!" Suddenly there was a stunned silence and the little boy found that hundreds of pairs of eyes were staring at him. Then someone sniggered . . . someone else tried to stifle a giggle . . . another person guffawed and snorted . . . and the whole crowd burst out into uncontrollable peals of laughter.

The emperor's face turned as red as a ripe tomato. "I am indeed a fool!" he murmured. "I have been swindled by two tricksters!" He ran back to the palace as fast as his short, naked legs could carry him – but the clever (and now very rich) weavers were long gone!

Blue Ribbons

Oh, dear, what can the matter be?
Oh, dear, what can the matter be?
Oh, dear, what can the matter be?
Johnny's so long at the fair.

He promised he'd buy me
a bunch of blue ribbons,
He promised he'd buy me
a bunch of blue ribbons,
He promised he'd buy me
a bunch of blue ribbons,
To tie up my bonny brown hair.

Ride a Cock-horse

Ride a cock-horse
to Banbury Cross,
To see a fine lady
upon a white horse;
Rings on her fingers
and bells on her toes,
She shall have music
wherever she goes.

Teddy Bear, Teddy Bear

Teddy bear, teddy bear, touch the ground.
Teddy bear, teddy bear, turn around.
Teddy bear, teddy bear, show your shoe
Teddy bear, teddy bear, that will do.
Teddy bear, teddy bear, run upstairs.
Teddy bear, teddy bear, say your prayers.
Teddy bear, teddy bear, blow out the light.
Teddy bear, teddy bear, Say GOODNIGHT.